Emma Memma Craft Book

This craft book belongs to

....

Ask a grown-up for help with cutting and the other tricky bits in these activities.

ACCORDION-FOLD FLUTTER AND FLY BUTTERFLIES!

Emma Memma is dancing in her flower garden with Flutter and Fly the Butterflies. Create your own butterflies and join in!

What you'll need for each butterfly:

1 piece of coloured paper

Scissors

Glue or sticky tape

Yarn/string/ribbon

Step 1:

Trace around the shapes below on your coloured paper, and then cut them out. The larger shape will form the top wings, the smaller shape the lower wings.

Step 2:

Taking one of the wings, fold a section lengthways, then flip the paper over and fold the same amount the other way. Keep the folds small and even, to create an accordion-look.

Step 3:

Repeat for the second wing.

Step 4:

To stick the wings together, place glue or sticky tape in a line on the top edge of the smaller wings. Then press down the larger wings on top so they are connected.

Step 5:

Next, take a short piece of yarn or string, and loop it around the centre part of the wings. Place each yarn-end at the top for the antennae and tie in a knot.

Step 6:

Now, carefully spread the folds of each wing, and add your finished butterfly to the flower garden you create on page 16. Make as many butterflies as you like!

PAPER-PLATE WAFFLES THE WOMBAT

Make your own Waffles the Wombat to sing, dance and sign with Emma Memma and Elvin Melvin to the 'Wombat Wednesday' song.

What you'll need:

1 large paper plate

1 small paper plate (if you only have large plates, you can cut around the edges to create a smaller circle)

Brown paint

Brown card (you can paint or colour plain paper or card to create this!)

Black felt or card

Thick-tipped black pen

Glue or sticky tape

Step 1:

Paint both plates brown. When the paint is dry, glue or sticky tape the smaller plate (the head) to the edge of the larger plate (the body).

Step 2:

Using scissors carefully cut out two small rectangles for the legs from the brown card. Also cut out two small triangles for the ears. Next, using the black felt or card, cut out two small circles for the eyes, and a slightly larger oval for the nose. You can draw them on instead if you prefer.

Step 3:

Glue or sticky tape the two brown triangles to the top of the small plate for your wombat's ears. Next, glue or sticky tape the two brown rectangles to the bottom of the large plate for the legs. Lastly, glue or sticky tape the two black circles to the upper face of the small plate for the eyes, and the oval below and centre for the nose. Then, using a black pen, draw a smiley mouth on your wombat.

CURLY WURLY

Emma Memma has bright red curly hair. Curls here, curls there! Make some red curls to add to the picture of Emma Memma below with glue or sticky tape.

There are several ways to make curls, so use one of the material options or all of them to create different curly textures!

What you'll need:

Thin strips of paper or thin ribbon or string or wool or twine

A long pencil or long paintbrush or straw

Red paint or marker pen

Step 1:

Grab the material you are using, and if it is not already red, paint it with the red paint (for paper, ribbon, wool or twine), or colour it in with your red marker pen (for paper or twine).

Step 2:

Once dry, take your thin piece of material and wind it around a long pencil or straw or the long handle of a paintbrush. Leave for a few hours.

Step 3:

Gently uncurl from your pencil and then cut to the desired length for Emma Memma's hair and stick it to the page. Don't forget to colour in Emma Memma!

POPSICLE-STICK GOATS

Emma Memma loves goats. They are one of her favourite animals. Go Go the Goats are playing on a hill, far out of town. Make your own goat ornaments from popsicle sticks.

What you'll need:

3 popsicle sticks
Glue
Brown paint
Thick-tipped black pen
Small pompom or bottle top
Cotton wool

Step 1:

Arrange your popsicle sticks into an upside-down triangle, then move the top stick down a bit to leave 2 horns at the top of the goat's head (see image below). Glue your popsicle sticks together (or you can use sticky tape if you prefer).

HOW TO ARRANGE YOUR POPSICLES

Step 2:

Once the glue has dried, paint the triangle brown.

Step 3:

Once the paint is dry, use the black pen to draw two eyes. Alternatively, stick on a pair of googly eyes.

Step 4:

Next, take a cotton-wool ball and pull it apart slightly so it looks more like hair. Stick the cotton wool to the underside of the bottom point of the triangle to make the goat's beard. Then stick the pompom or bottle top on the top side for the goat's nose.

TWIRLY TUESDAY TWIRLERS

Emma Memma and her mates love to twirl, especially on Twirly Tuesday! You can twirl with your body, your arms or make a special twirler too. You can also decorate your twirler with butterflies and hearts and swirls and twirls, or a rainbow of colours.

What you'll need:

Paper
Coloured pens
Scissors
Glue
String

Step 1:

Draw 2 circles the same size, about 12cm across, like the size of an orange. Decorate them and colour them in. The more colourful, the better!

Step 2:

Using scissors, carefully cut out the two circles. Then, glue the backs of the two circles together to make one colourful circle.

Step 3:

Using a pencil or your scissors, make a small hole in the centre of the circle. Then, cut a long length of string, and thread it through your twirler. Tie the string ends together, and spin your twirler! Once the string gets wound up tight, it will spin faster and easier.

PEBBLE PEOPLE

Emma likes to take twirly walks to look at all the amazing plants, flowers and insects in her garden. With a grown-up, go on a twirly tour of your garden, park or pathway and collect some flat pebbles to make your own Emma Memma and Elvin Melvin.

What you'll need:

4 flat pebbles (2 large oval, 2 small round)

Pencil

Different coloured acrylic paint

Step 1:

Wash and dry the pebbles to remove any dirt.

Step 2:

Using a pencil or paint or any other craft item you might have, draw a face and hair on each of the two round pebbles for Emma Memma and Elvin Melvin. Remember to give Emma Memma lots of curls!

Step 3:

On the 2 large oval pebbles, draw the clothes for Emma Memma's and Elvin Melvin's bodies.

You could also create pebble animals or butterflies too!

Step 4:

When the paint is dry, place the heads and bodies together and display them for your friends and family to see.

EMMA MEMMA'S COLOURFUL POP-UP CARD

Do you like making things for your family and friends? Join Emma Memma and create a colourful pop-up card that you can give to someone special.

What you'll need:

Piece of coloured cardboard

2 pieces of paper

Ruler

Coloured pencils or marker pens

Glue

Step 1:

Fold your piece of cardboard in half – this will be the base of your card.

Step 2:

Grab one of your pieces of A4 paper and, measuring along the short edge of the paper, measure 10cm from the edge and mark with a dot. Do the same on the other short edge and then draw a line between the two dots. Cut along the line.

Step 3:

Take the smaller strip of paper and, using the marker pens or pencils, colour a finger length of a single colour. Then use another colour to do the same and another, until the paper is all coloured in.

Step 4:

Fold one of the short edges of the paper back by about a finger width. Then flip the paper over and fold the paper again by the same width. Continue until you have folded all of the paper like an accordion.

Step 5:

Open the base card and then glue one edge of the accordion paper to the left side of the card - make sure the rainbow colour is facing towards you. Then glue down the other edge of the accordion paper to the right-side of the card.

Step 6:

Take your second piece of paper and place over the cloud shape on the opposite page or the butterfly shape on page 14. Trace these to make your own clouds and butterflies. Colour them in, then cut them out and glue to your card.

Step 7:

Add your message to the card and any other drawings you might want to include. Happy days!

RAINBOW COLLAGE

Elvin Melvin wears green overalls and an orange-and-pink shirt. He likes all sorts of colours so his favourite thing in the sky is a rainbow. Can you make a collage rainbow too?

What you'll need:

A piece of paper or card

Pencil

Scissors

Unwanted paper products like magazines, mail brochures, catalogues or old wrapping paper

Glue

Step 1:

Draw the arched shape of a rainbow on your paper or card – it can be as big as you like. Cut out the rainbow.

Step 2:

Cut up your paper into different shapes at different sizes – the more colourful the better.

Step 3:

Arrange your paper shapes onto the rainbow and create a pattern with the colours in any way you want. You could put similar colours together or scatter them around to make a colourful picture. Once you're happy with the layout of your rainbow, glue the colourful shapes to the large rainbow.

Step 4:

Display your rainbow by sticking it on the fridge or on your bedroom window!

ELVIN MELVIN'S FLYING GREEN PLANE

Build your own green plane and zoom it through the air!

What you'll need:

Scissors

Glue

Step 1:

Ask a grown-up to help you pull out these two pages from the staples. Using scissors, carefully cut along the dotted line around each part of the plane. There are three parts to the plane: the body, the wings and the tail. Remember to cut along the dotted lines in the middle of the body and at the ends, too. This can be a bit tricky, so you might need a grown-up to help you.

Step 2:

Using the fold that is already along the body of the plane, fold it in half and glue the two sides together. The 'holes' you have cut on each side should line up.

Step 3:

Slot the wings through the central hole of the body, and the tail through the cut on the end.

Step 4:

Fly your plane!

GARDEN GRAZING

Goats like to eat almost anything. They especially love grass and dandelion flowers. Grab a bowl from your kitchen and create a special lunch for Go Go the Goats with things from your garden or the local park. Some things goats like to eat are below:

Grass	Leaves
Flowers	Bark
Apples	Carrots

What are your favourite foods? Draw some of them below. Yum!

BUTTERFLY CLIPS

Did you know that a group of butterflies is called a flutter, a flight or a kaleidoscope? Let's make some butterfly clips that you can wear or decorate your house with!

What you'll need:

- A piece of paper
- Colouring pencils or marker pens
- Scissors
- Sticky tape
- Hairclips, bobby pins or paperclips

Step 1:

Place your piece of paper over one of the butterfly shapes below. Trace the butterfly shape and then colour it in. Maybe your butterfly will have green spots or colourful stripes – or perhaps they're orange and pink like Flutter and Fly!

Step 2:

Cut out your butterfly and stick it to the clip you're using with sticky tape.

Step 3:

Clip the butterfly to your shirt or your bag or your hair (but be careful not to use the paperclips in hair as these can get tangled).

INDOOR GARDEN FUN

Rain, rain, go away! Sometimes it's lovely to look at a garden when you're inside - especially if it's raining outdoors. You can create a colourful garden that is perfect for you to play with your butterflies from page 2.

What you'll need:

- A piece of paper
- Reusable tack
- Cardboard (thick card is good so you can use an old box or another reused card item)
- Paper straw or chopstick or wooden spoon
- Sticky tape
- Coloured string or ribbon
- Jar or other container like an old plastic pot or yoghurt container
- Dirt or sand or pebbles or scrunched up newspaper or magazines

Step 1:

Place the paper over one of the flower shapes and trace around it.

Step 2:

Roughly cut out the flower shape and tack it to your cardboard. Cut the flower shape neatly so you have a lovely cardboard flower. Keep the paper flower to make more!

Step 3:

Sticky tape the flower to the top of a paper straw or whatever you're using for the stem of the plant.

Step 4:

Gather the coloured string or ribbon and wrap the string around the flower from the bottom to the top and continue until there's lots of colour on your flower - like in the picture. Tie a knot in your string and then cut off the end.

Step 5:

Get the container you are using and wrap string or ribbon around the top of the container several times, then tie a bow with both ends.

Step 6:

To create the base for the flower to sit in, grab whatever you are using like dirt, sand or scrunched up paper and place it in the bottom of the container, filling it almost to the top. Then gently insert the stem of your flower into the base to complete your beautiful garden!

EMMA MEMMA AND FRIENDS FIGURINES

Create these fun figurines and twirl and jump with Emma Memma and her friends.

Make sure you read the other side of the next page before you start cutting.

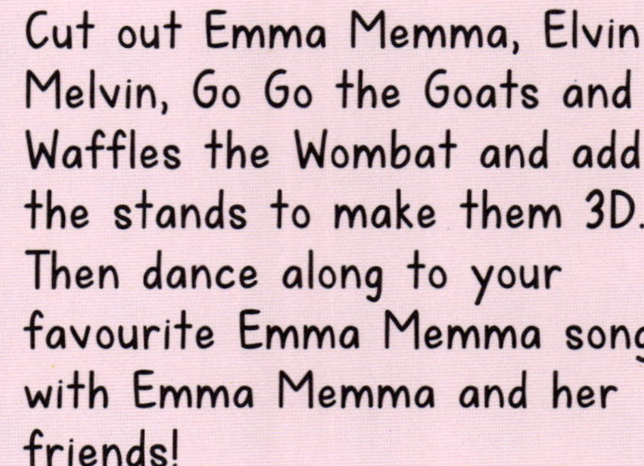

Cut out Emma Memma, Elvin Melvin, Go Go the Goats and Waffles the Wombat and add the stands to make them 3D. Then dance along to your favourite Emma Memma song with Emma Memma and her friends!

FUN FACTS

Did you know?

Wombats are marsupials and the females have a pouch for their young.

Did you know?

Goats have great balance and are wonderful climbers.

Did you know?

Australian native bees are a variety of colours – some are black and yellow, others have brown, red or green colouring or even blue dots!

Did you know?

Butterflies taste with their feet.

Did you know?

Goats don't have teeth on their upper jaw – instead they have a strong dental plate for chewing their food.

Did you know?

Wombats can run as fast as humans.

Did you know?

A group of wombats is called a wisdom of wombats or a colony of wombats or a mob of wombats.

PETAL PRESSING

Help Emma Memma and her friends to capture some of the beauty of nature. Collect amazing flowers and leaves from your backyard or park and press them flat to use in a decoration of your choice.

What you'll need:

Small flowers and leaves – make sure you pick flowers that don't belong to someone else, or ask their permission first

2 pieces of paper

Lots of heavy books

Step 1:

Place one of the pieces of paper on top of a heavy book like a cookbook or textbook – a book with a hard cover is best. Space out the flowers or leaves on top of the paper, then cover with the second piece of paper.

Step 2:

Grab another heavy book and gently put it on top, flattening the flowers and leaves.

Step 3:

Carefully move the books to a place where you will be able to leave them for a few days to a week. Then put even more books on top to add extra weight to your press.

Step 4:

After a few days or a week, gently remove the top books, then slowly lift off the piece of paper that is on top of your flowers. Your flowers and leaves should be nice and flat but still have their lovely colour.

Step 5:

Use your flowers to create a twirly card (by gluing them to some cardboard) or create a lovely hanging decoration (by placing the flowers and leaves in between two pieces of clear contact and then adding some string or ribbon).

WHIRLING WHEEL

Make a colourful pinwheel and watch it twirl in the wind! See if it moves as you dance.

What you'll need:

Paper

Scissors

Pencils or marker pens

Glue

A tack or sewing pin

A paper straw

Step 1:

Place your paper over the square shape and circle on the next page and trace the lines of the shapes – don't forget the dotted lines – and the small circle.

Step 2:

Cut out your square. Use your pencils or marker pens to colour both sides of the square. You can use whatever colours you would like – Emma Memma likes orange and pink.

Step 3:

Cut along the dotted lines. Looking at the template, take one of the corners where an 'F' is marked and glue it to the centre cross 'x'. Then do the same for the other three corners.

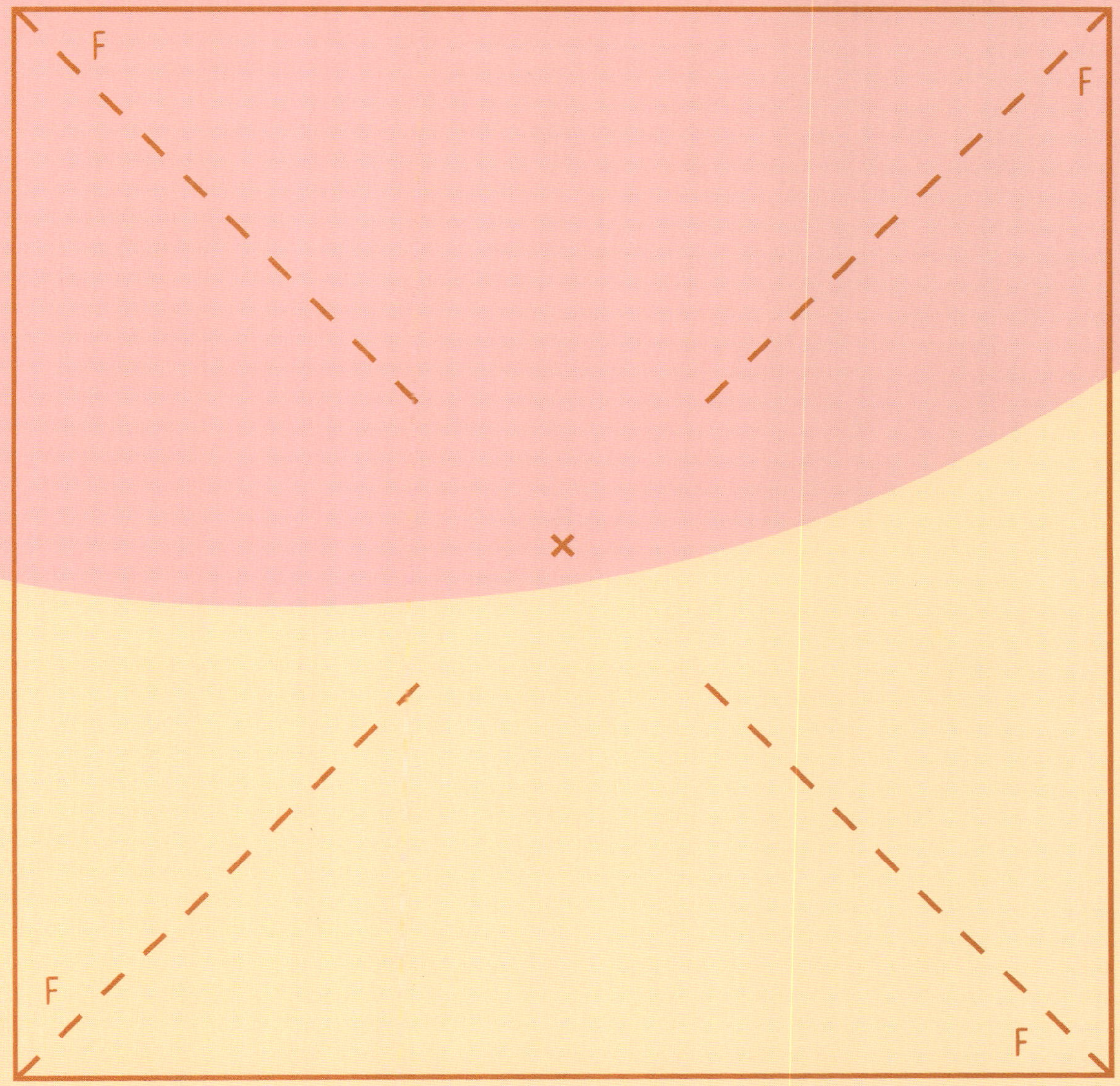

F

F

F

F

Step 4:

Cut out the circle and then, with the help of a grown-up, push the pin or tack you are using through the centre of the circle. Then place the pin through the centre of the wheel you have created.

Step 5:

Grab the straw and push the pin through the top of the straw to secure the wheel to the handle. You can also use a chopstick or stick you've found in the garden, instead. Place some reusable tack on the pointy bit of the pin to make it safe. If you're using a stick, you will need to sticky tape the pin to the top of it.

SPOT THE DIFFERENCE

Waffles the Wombat and Go Go the Goats are playing in the garden. Can you circle the three differences between the pictures?

ANSWERS: 1. Missing butterfly 2. Missing bee 3. Missing grass